I Was Ten Years Old When I Went For A Walk

John Anderson

© 2023 by John Anderson. All rights reserved.

Words Matter Publishing
P.O. Box 1190
Decatur, IL 62525
www.wordsmatterpublishing.com

ISBN: 978-1-958-00042-7

Library of Congress Catalog Card Number: 2023938307

Dedication

This book is dedicated to my wife and partner, Kathy. Without her constant will to fight, I would not have survived as long as I have. She has made endless doctor appointments, runs to the drug store, scheduled MRIs, and driven me to the hospital for daily radiation therapy, chemotherapy, and clinical trials. Kathy also arranged all of our travel on multiple occasions to Gainesville, FL, Rochester, MN, and Nashville, TN, all while keeping our house running, staying in touch with our children, and helping them with their lives. She has only let me see her cry a couple of times during all of this, 99% of the time, she holds my hand, gives me a big hug, and looks at me with love in her eyes. After Christ, she is the greatest gift God has given me.

Acknowledgments

I want to thank all of my doctors who have monitored and managed my case: Dr. Meyer (Mayo Clinic, Rochester), Dr. Tran and Dr. Ghiaseddin (UF Shand's), Phuong, who ran the trial at Shand's, Dr. Merrell (Vanderbilt) and Dr. Buchanan.

I would also like to express my sincere gratitude to my family and friends, who stood by us and encouraged me to keep fighting, prayed for us, and sent us emails, texts, letters, cards, and food to keep our spirits up.

My brother, Stuart, helped us navigate Mayo Clinic, and my brother, Richard, helped us with critical decisions. My children, Preston and Raye, and my son-in-law, Noah. My parents and grandchildren, Jonah, and James, for giving me a reason to fight.

My sister-in-law, Susan, paid our bills and helped run our house when Kathy couldn't. Kathy's brother, Raymond, ensured we got where we needed to go at a high personal cost. Maria, who got our mail; my sister-in-law, Cindy, who fed us some wonderful meatloaf; and Berdette, who visited us in Florida.

Mary Lou and Aunt Ann gave me constant encouragement. My friend, Rodney drove me to church every Sunday, and my friend Bill, whose strength inspires me. Last but not least, Kathy's sister, Annie, and her husband, John, put up with us for over a year in Florida cheerleading all the way! I thank their friends, BJ and Jamie, for putting us up in their home. My friend, Dr. Jerry Thompson, called me weekly with a new joke for a good laugh!

I am thankful for God, who gave me Christ, and all these wonderful people and events in my life. I am even grateful for the cancer that helped me see how many blessings God has given me.

Table of Contents

Introduction

This book is about God's constant presence in your life and how He continues to bless you during your trials. If you are reading this, it is because I was diagnosed with a terminal illness. While going through treatments, I asked God what I should do with my "between" time. The time between radiation, chemotherapy, and clinical trials. The doctor had suggested woodworking, but I didn't think I was ready yet for a new hobby that included sharp knives.

I kept asking God, and finally, I heard in my head, "try writing." It sounded much safer than woodworking. I'd never written anything other than business letters and emails. I had never considered writing a book. So, I started writing, relying on God to guide me. What I hoped to get out of it was a fun project that would lead to other fun projects. I also hoped to help others with the mental and spiritual struggles we face during times of tragedy.

In the same way, God gave me the title, which is basically about my faith walk with God. These are just a few of the stories from my life where I felt God's presence and direct involvement in my life. I'm sure anyone reading this has similar stories from their own lives. Many people would say that isn't God; that's just happenstance. Next time one of these stories happen in your life, reflect on it. Take some time, and think of the wonder and majesty of God while you do.

Jesus is the light of the world. Realize without light, there truly is nothing. Without God, life has no meaning. Being thankful for the time God spends with you and the gifts He is constantly delivering to you will build your faith and lead you to His comfort, peace, and joy.

CHAPTER 1

Decisions

I had just had what medical science considers a terminal (glioblastoma) tumor removed from my brain. Not only is such a tumor regarded as "terminal," mine had the special characteristic of being "non-methylated," which meant the standard treatment used for prolonging life would be less effective.

My wife, Kathy, and I had to make a decision about where to go for treatment (radiation and chemotherapy). I pushed for the Mayo Clinic in Jacksonville, Florida, but Kathy wasn't sure it was the right place. Becoming upset, I insisted that she decide where to go. Since it was a fast-growing cancer, time was critical. But instead of continuing to pressure my wife, I went for a walk. That I could walk, I suddenly realized, was blessing number one. In spite of the fact that I had a tumor about the size of a baseball surgically removed from my brain, I could still walk! Furthermore, I could also talk, have conversations, and see pretty well (though I had lost 30 percent of my left peripheral vision).

During the entire walk, all I could think about was how Kathy was panicking, but she had to make a decision soon. I begged God to help us.

When I returned home, I encountered my next blessing. Kathy was waiting at the door. Giving me a big hug, she said, "We are going to Gainesville!"

The doctors at the Mayo Clinic in Rochester (where my surgery had taken place) had highly recommended Dr. David Tran, the head of neuro-oncology at the University of Florida. During my walk, Kathy had been on the phone with her sister, Annie. She lived in Gainesville with her husband, John, and had previously mentioned that the University of Florida has an excellent neurological hospital. Annie suggested we ask the physicians in Rochester if Gainesville would be a good choice for my treatments.

Also, while I was on my walk, Annie contacted a friend of hers. The woman-owned a house in Gainesville that she wasn't currently living in, and it was just across from Annie's. After hearing about our situation, her friend immediately told Annie that we could stay at her house. We ended up remaining there for eight months, and she and her husband have told us the house is ours to use anytime we need it. What a blessing this was in the middle of our emotional storm. It felt like a gift straight from God.

Such are the blessings that I have found throughout my life, blessings I want to share with you on these pages. They often came in the most unusual forms and in the most unexpected places. May my experiences help you to recognize similar blessings in your own lives.

CHAPTER 2

Treatment

We headed to Gainesville, where we first met Dr. Tran. Although we didn't know it at the time, medical research had been currently developing a vaccine to fight my type of cancer. The only place in the country where the clinical trial for the vaccine was accepting new patients was Gainesville, God had led us there via Annie and her friend. Duke University had also been running a trial but couldn't accept new patients because of a shortage of supply for the new medication.

Dr. Tran mentioned that the trial in Gainesville might be accepting new patients and asked if I would be interested. I said, "Sure!" When one of the nurses mentioned that she thought they had stopped enrolling new patients, Dr. Tran made a phone call to find out. Fortunately, they were still accepting new patients and would include me.

Before entering the trial, each patient must complete Standard of Care (SOC) treatments. The next day I was getting fitted for my radiation helmet. It holds your head in a fixed position while you receive six weeks of daily SOC radiation treatments.

We (I say we because Kathy was there every step of the way) then started the SOC treatments which also included daily chemotherapy.

John and Annie took their roles seriously. They saw to it that we were fed and entertained every day. Usually, we would just grab a bite to eat while they would crack jokes, keeping our spirits up. John also took turns with Kathy to go with me on three or four-mile walks every day. Sometimes he would accompany me for a second jaunt in the afternoon. I figure I've walked more than 1,100 miles since this started.

Friends would send emails, texts, cards, and letters or make phone calls telling us they were praying for us. I have one friend who has called or texted at least once a week and often more frequently to ask how I'm doing and let me know he is still praying for me! Many of those messages would arrive just when we needed them most.

For example, Kathy had just driven us from Gainesville to Kentucky. Before the tumor, I always drove. A tough drive through the mountains of east Tennessee made Kathy nervous! (FYI, she is an excellent driver). We arrived after a stressful 11-hour drive. Part of the stress resulted from the fact that I was in the middle of weaning myself off of an anxiety medicine. Worn out and depressed, we carried our bags into the house and saw a large stack of mail in the kitchen. I noticed, in particular, one from David, a friend I used to work with. Still having trouble reading, I asked Kathy if she would read it to me. We sat on our bed, and Kathy started reading, then we both started laughing. It got to the point where we had tears of joy running down our cheeks. David's letter was twelve pages long and full of funny stories about old friends and situations we had gotten ourselves into through the years.

Although David had written his letter three months before, it hadn't been forwarded to us in Florida. God saw to it that we received it at just the right time! Our doom and gloom had been turned on its head to joy! During this period, we frequently received gifts like this from God.

How much more evidence do you need that God does exist? Three months prior, an old friend had taken the time to write a twelve-page letter meant to cheer me up. It failed to get forwarded to us in Florida, and after eight months away and a stressful 11- hour drive home from treatment, it was there sitting prominently in a stack of mail, waiting for us on the kitchen table. Delivered with God's perfect timing!

CHAPTER 3

Imperfect Faith

You may be wondering what the title of my memoirs has to do with my story. When I was ten years old, I came to faith in Christ. As a young boy, I would often go for walks and then shoot basketballs in the driveway hoop. On this particular day, I was taking shots further and further away to see how far I could hurl the ball. Having recently been thinking about God, I began to wonder how one knows whether He is real or not. I thought if I could just know, it would solve all my concerns about life and, worst of all, the fear of death. I had just reached the end of our driveway and couldn't get any farther from the basketball goal when an idea came to me.

I knew I couldn't shoot the ball so far with two hands. But I might be able to throw it with one hand. Suddenly I prayed, "God, if you make this basketball go in when I throw it all the way from here, I will know you are real." Backing up into the street, I took a running start, then threw the ball one-handed as hard as I could toward the basket. The ball went "SWISH" and through the net!

Shocked, I should have immediately fallen to my knees in prayer and thanked God for the confirmation of His existence! But that's not what I did. Instead, I grabbed the ball and started negotiating with Him. "God, that was amazing, and I'm sure you are real, but if you will do it just one more time. then I will be absolutely, positively sure!" Well, I took another long throw at the basket and didn't get close. At first, I was pretty disappointed. Then I got to thinking about how amazing that first shot had been. I thought God just had to be real, that there was no way I could have made that shot without His help. So, I decided to accept Christ as my Savior and keep working on my faith. I have experienced many of God's blessings, whether they were something I begged Him to deliver or were His many free gifts, such as sunsets, waterfalls, or the smile of a one-year-old grandchild. I could insist on absolute perfect evidence of God's existence, or I can open my eyes to the evidence that He has provided me and accept my imperfect faith made perfect through Christ.

Through the years, I found my faith was there to guide me as well as strengthen my testimony in the words of God.

CHAPTER 4

Second Chance

Lying in the MRI machine, I wondered what was wrong. Recently I had been having problems with my vision, bumping into things on my left, and having trouble getting numbers correct on spreadsheets at the office. When I went to the optometrist, they tested my eyes and said, "Everything is perfect." My retinas were good, the lenses clear, etc.

"No, it isn't," I protested, "there is definitely something wrong!"

The optometrist suggested that he could do a visual field test, whatever that was. "Okay, let's do that," I replied. She told me that while they didn't have time that day if I came back tomorrow, they would do it then.

The next day a technician took me to a room occupied by a large white globe with a place for your head. The tech ran the test, then said, "We better do this again." So, she did. When I asked her about the results, she replied that normally the doctor would discuss the results with the patient, but since the optometrist was out of town, she commented that I should probably see an ophthalmologist. When I phoned Kathy and told her, she called Dr. Haleman, who had just done her cataract surgery, and he told her to bring me to his office at nine the next morning.

We arrived early, and Dr. Helman saw me right away. He looked at the test results and then had his technician run another field test on me. Afterward, Dr. Helman came into the room and told us he thought I was having a stroke or had one. Then he recommended that we go to the emergency room and get an MRI. He said he would have the physician in charge of the ER meet me at the entrance.

The ER doctor led me to a technician who started the MRI process. Initially, I thought to myself that people have strokes all the time and often survive them with just minor complications. Perhaps I would have to start taking blood thinners or something like that. But as I laid there, I started thinking, "Maybe this is serious." I might not get to watch my grandchildren grow up. Suddenly I started to pray, "God, please give me a second chance. I'll do better."

In my thoughts, I heard God say, "What's wrong with now!" At first, I felt confused, but then I realized that He was telling me I should be thankful now. As I lay there in the machine begging for my second chance, I looked up and saw a sunlit multicolored plastic sign hanging from the ceiling. It wasn't particularly beautiful by the world's standards, but at the time, it was one of the most striking things I had ever seen.

Instantly I realized that God had given me a second chance. I started looking at things differently. Staring at that plastic sign in awe of the beauty that God had bestowed on it, I thanked Him for the new realization. I thanked Him for the light that shone through the sign in such a wonderful way. I thanked Him for the people who made the plastic sign so that I could see it. Finally, thanking Him for the ability to see it, I started to feel joy.

We were waiting on the results when the physician walked in and told us I had a brain tumor.

CHAPTER 5

The Hotel

My younger brother took several days off work to accompany us to the Mayo Clinic and help Kathy and I get around, carry bags, etc., after the surgery to remove the tumor. It was a huge blessing and relief for me to know that my wife wouldn't have to deal with everything by herself. When we checked into the hotel, we went to the room and immediately noticed that it had no exterior windows to let light in. The room was dark. Not liking it, Kathy went to the front desk to see if we could get another room. The clerk explained that no other rooms were available since the hotel was full.

After getting some dinner, we went to bed. The next day we decided to walk to St. Mary's Church which is attached to the hospital and was supposed to be beautiful. And it was beautiful. While we were there, a nun approached my wife and asked about us. Kathy told her about my upcoming surgery. The nun gave her a hug and said that she would pray for us continuously for two weeks. We thought it was a wonderful gesture, thanked her, and started to head back to the hotel.

On the way, Kathy pointed out what appeared to be a brand-new hotel with ground-to-roof glass walls. Then she asked if we could stop in there and see if they had any rooms. My brother and I both said "no." My surgery was the next morning, we were tired, and I didn't want to pack up and move. Kathy pleaded and said it wouldn't hurt to look.

The lobby was a wide-open space with lots of light and a really cheery atmosphere. Not only did the hotel have rooms available, but they were also half the price of the hotel we were staying in. The staff told us that a doctor from the Mayo Clinic had built it. He understood what patients had to deal with when coming to the clinic, and he wanted to provide a hotel with a bright open interior with plenty of room to walk, reasonably priced, and conveniently right across from the hospital. It felt like another gift delivered directly from God or from Him due to Kathy's persistence. My brother Stuart and I both agreed we had been wrong and headed to get our bags and check out of the other hotel.

CHAPTER 6

Kathy

I was twelve years old when Kathy and I were on the same swim team. Since she was two years older than me, she had no interest (she didn't know I existed), and I had no shot at getting her attention. She was nice enough to me in a mothering way.

Fast forward a few years, I had graduated from the University of Kentucky with a degree in business. Having completed a degree in education from Western Kentucky, she would soon have a job teaching first grade. I was living in North Carolina, working for a developer. The owner of the development company had been a real blessing to me. He gave me my first job out of school and taught me how to make a living for myself and my future family. He called and told me he wanted me to return to Kentucky for another assignment. I packed all my worldly possessions into a small U-Haul trailer and headed out.

My parents let me move back in with them until I could get my own place. Upon my arrival, the first thing my mother said to me (after the hug and kiss) was she had met the most beautiful girl that day at the endodontist. She went on about her pretty face, almond-shaped brown eyes, cute figure, sweet personality, etc., and said I had to meet her.

After a few obligatory "Okays," I made my escape and headed out to a restaurant to meet a friend of mine.

There, he said, "Hey, man, I know this girl, and I think you guys would really hit it off. Want me to call her and see if she will come to meet us?"

Kathy did, and we did hit it off. Turns out she was the same beautiful girl my mother had met earlier that day. If your mother has a good relationship with Christ (she does), and she wants you to meet a girl, you might as well go ahead and do it.

I made Kathy laugh a few times, and she told me she had a horse called Alphie that she stabled not far from where we were. Would I like to go see him?

"Sure," I said. We had a good time petting and feeding Alphie, which I'm sure was a test I had to pass. Then I drove her back to her car, and we said goodbye.

The next day I got Kathy's address from my friend and decided to just drop by and knock on the door unannounced. When she opened the door, I saw this amazingly beautiful girl. I had caught her off guard, so she had absolutely zero makeup on and was wearing a grey flannel sweatshirt and old blue jeans. Right then, I decided I was going to marry her. I figured if she was this beautiful with no makeup, wearing jeans and an old grey sweatshirt, and didn't yell at me to go away, she was my kind of girl.

Turns out Kathy isn't only pretty and sweet; she is also tough. God couldn't have given me a more perfect mate to help me navigate through all the doctors' appointments and blood draws, MRI scans, chemo, radiation, etc. I would face in the future. I don't know how I would have made it to this point without her. She is a blessing that I am thankful for every day. I proposed to Kathy on a school day while she was teaching her first-grade class. The kids loved it! I learned later that day after I left that she had gone running down the hallway yelling to all the other teachers that I had proposed. I was happy to learn Kathy was as excited about marrying me as I was about her.

CHAPTER 7

Dr. Dang

Kathy and I were on our honeymoon in Hawaii. My cousin and her husband were stationed there with the Navy. They asked us to have dinner with them at a national chain Mexican restaurant. We had a healthy appetite and ate a nice meal. Later that night, Kathy started feeling nauseous at about 10:00 pm. I heard her yelling for me to help her in the bathroom. As I opened the door, she shouted, "No, no, close the door."

A few minutes later, she wanted me back to help, then exclaimed, "No, shut the door."

This went on for about 10 minutes until she came out of the bathroom. Obviously, she had food poisoning. Though dumbfounded, I, of course, started praying, kind of begging God to help me. I didn't know what to do. She was violently ill. After another bout in the bathroom, I called the front desk. It was a Sunday evening, and we were in an unfamiliar place. I told them what was going on and asked if they had a house doctor or knew of anyone who could assist us.

"No, sorry," they replied.

Kathy then said to call her Uncle Bill. Kathy's father died when she was one year old, and Uncle Bill was the closest thing she had had to a father while she was growing up.

"What can Uncle Bill do for us on a Sunday night 4,000 miles away in Kentucky?" I questioned.

It turned out that he could do a lot. I got him on the phone and told him what was happening. He said, "Let me hang up, and I'll call you back." A few minutes later, the phone rang, and on it was Dr. Dang. He told me he would be right over to pick us up and that he would be driving a blue Lincoln. We were to meet him out front.

After grabbing Kathy's purse, we headed downstairs, with me steadying her. Dr. Dang was the head surgeon at the Honolulu Hospital, and he and Uncle Bill had been roommates in medical school. He drove us right up to the emergency room. They already had a gurney waiting for Kathy. Dr. Dang immediately had an IV in Kathy to get fluids back in her and an anti-nausea drug. In no time at all, she was feeling good and chatting it up with the nurses and Dr. Dang. Here we were, 4,000 miles from home on a Sunday evening, being cared for by a top surgeon.

By the way, it was now early morning, and we had a flight back to California that day. "Don't worry about it," Dr. Dang assured us, "I'll make sure you get to the airport." He drove us back to the hotel, where we got our bags, and then he delivered us to the airport with time to spare.

God doesn't always answer our prayers the way we want. Sometimes the answer is "No." This time, however, the answer was definitely, "I'll take care of it."

On the flight back to California, after the flight crew had just served a meal, Kathy was still a little queasy and feeling the effects of the food poisoning. She wanted to get up and head to the bathroom. As she stepped into the aisle, she fainted and fell across the aisle onto another passenger's food tray. The tray had metal arms on it that acted like springs. The food went flying as the spring arms slung it toward the ceiling and then onto several other passengers as she rolled off the first passenger and his tray into the aisle. She ended up flat on her back, out cold.

I started yelling, "Is there a doctor on the plane?" (I think I had seen this in a movie or something), all the while worrying that I was going to have to start dating again. (Seriously, the thought went through my head). But I was also praying that Kathy was okay.

When I looked down, I saw a man leaning over my wife, talking to her. It was the doctor I had shouted out for. He worked with the stewardess getting Kathy back to consciousness. Within a few minutes, she was once again in her seat, sitting next to me and doing better. The rest of the flight was pretty uneventful. Another prayer had been answered.

CHAPTER 8

Lips

I was in the second grade when my Aunt Nancy asked me to help her get a picture of her German Shepherd, Brutus. The dog was pretty mean. His favorite pastime was chasing the mailman and occasionally getting a small bite. Unfortunately, his habit was getting out of hand, and Aunt Nancy decided Brutus needed to go to a new family out in the country. She had a small camera (it was before cell phones) and decided to take a picture of the animal to advertise him.

She put Brutus on his leash, but he tugged, jumped, and barked the entire time. Finally, my aunt said, "John, why don't you take the picture, and I'll hold Brutus. That way, I can be in the picture with him."

I reached over for the camera just as Brutus jumped up and bit the left half of my upper lip off. Aunt Nancy screamed, got Brutus under control, and ran me inside the house to get some ice and a towel to stop the bleeding. Pressing the ice against my lip, she loaded me in her Volkswagen Beetle, and we raced to the hospital. What I remember about the drive was feeling a little woozy and reading all the billboards and other signs on the way. I was seven and thought I was doing a pretty good job of being able to read everything we passed.

When we reached the hospital, the head of surgery happened to be there. And they immediately took me to an operating room, where he sewed my lip back together. During a follow-up visit, I learned it had taken thirty-seven stitches to do the job. It turned out that the surgeon was Uncle Bill—my future wife Kathy's Uncle Bill. Later I would thank him for saving my lip so that I could kiss his niece with it, (one of my favorite pastimes). Kathy would just roll her eyes when I said it and occasionally tell him she appreciated it too. Good thing God's plan didn't include Brutus swallowing my lip!

God works in mysterious ways.

CHAPTER 9

Plastic Roast

Kathy and I both lived in Kentucky and had been dating for several weeks when she said that she and her friend Brenda would like to make dinner for my friend, Craig and me. Would I see if I could get him to come?

My wife loves to play matchmaker. I tend to stay out of the way when she starts matchmaking, but we had only been dating a few weeks at this point, and I was crazy about her, so I said I would give it a try. Craig reluctantly agreed to come.

He and I were sitting in the living room talking when we heard some noise and laughter in the kitchen. We also smelled a hint of smoke. Exchanging glances, we just continued our conversation. About ten minutes later, Kathy and Brenda summoned us to the table.

For some reason, they kept looking at each other and giggling. They brought a beautiful roast to the table along with salads. Kathy took a serving knife and placed nice portions on each of our plates. Because they kept grinning at each other and giggling, Craig and I were a little suspicious and hadn't started in on the meal. "Why aren't you eating?" Kathy asked.

"Why are you giggling?" we asked back.

"Oh, Brenda just told me a funny story."

Accepting this, we dug in. We both took a bite of roast and started chewing. Initially, it tasted pretty good, but it was tough, so Craig and I both kept chewing and chewing and chewing. Finally, we both took the meat out of our mouths and set it on the plate. Kathy and Brenda thought this was hilarious. At this point, Craig and I started laughing but didn't know why.

In a few minutes, we were all laughing. It went on for a good ten minutes until Kathy finally confessed. She told us they had used the wrong type of plastic cooking bag. When they noticed, it had started melting onto the roast. That had been when Craig and I had first heard the noise and giggling in the kitchen. They had started trying to get the plastic off the roast but couldn't remove it all. Not knowing what to do and having nothing else they could serve, they decided a little plastic wouldn't hurt anyone. After all, it really didn't look that bad, so they called us to the table for dinner. Thankfully God had given Craig and me sense enough to spit it out and not swallow it!

CHAPTER 10

Rough Sailing

Because my father loved sailing, as a result, so did I. Unfortunately, my mother couldn't stand it. For her, it is like camping but much more uncomfortable. Her idea of roughing it is staying at a hotel with a credit card.

Regardless, my dad spent most of his adult life trying to make or acquire a sailboat that he thought would check all the comfort boxes for my mother. What he didn't realize was that it wasn't so much the boat that she objected to as the way he sailed it. My dad always loved to test the limits, whether it was how much sail the boat could carry in a certain wind or how shallow a channel we could squeeze through. His hobby led to some interesting experiences for our family.

One particularly windy day, we had gone sailing on Kentucky Lake with my brothers and some friends of my parents (Peggy and John Brown). The wind was howling, and we were moving along briskly under full sail. The waves splashing over the lower railing on the deck soaked everything.

Understandably not happy, my mother whispered into Peggy's ear to follow her below deck into the galley, where the two of them proceeded to make Bloody Marys. They just about had the blender full of Bloody Mary mix when the boat came to a screeching halt. Everything that wasn't tied down went flying. The TV flashed by my mother's face and hit Mrs. Brown in the back of her head. When Mrs. Brown fell down on a bunk, holding her head and crying that she was bleeding, my mother grabbed a towel and started wiping the blood out of Mrs. Brown's hair so that she could see the wound.

As she cleansed the wound, my mother suddenly stuck a couple of her bloody fingers in her mouth and told Mrs. Brown she should be okay, that it wasn't blood in her hair but instead the drink mix.

The bigger problem was that we were no longer moving. The boat had run up on a tree stump that must have been at least seven feet in diameter. After about five minutes, while my dad was trying to figure out how to get us underway again, my mother came up from the galley to let us know they were going to be okay.

But the problem remained that we were in the middle of Kentucky Lake, stuck on a stump. We had all the sail up, trying to get the boat to lean (heel) over enough so that it would slide off the stump. Unfortunately, it didn't work. If we used the sails to turn the boat, the vessel would just pivot on the stump.

Finally, my dad had my older brother and me get in the tiny inflatable dinghy with its five-horsepower motor. We had a line (halyard) tied to the top of the forty-foot-tall mast.

Mr. Brown jumped in the water to help my brother and me secure the halyard to the back of the dinghy. As soon as he did, the wind and waves started carrying him, my brother, me, and the dinghy away from the boat. The idea was to use the leverage of the mast by pulling it with the dinghy to heel the boat over far enough to get us loose from the stump. What could possibly go wrong?

Of course, my older brother, Richard, got the job driving the dingy. My responsibility was to shift my weight around the dinghy in an effort to keep us from flipping over. Mr. Brown's task was to survive the swim back to the boat after he got the line secured to the dinghy. As he swam furiously against the wind and waves, my mother and Mrs. Brown stood on the boat screaming and crying for him to swim harder. After about ten minutes of championship swimming and the women coming unglued, Mr. Brown suddenly stood up.

He had discovered that the water where we were stuck was only about three feet deep. Casually Mr. Brown waded the rest of the way to the sailboat and climbed aboard to the great relief of Mrs. Brown and my mother.

My dad had the sail completely up and hollered for Richard to start pulling with the dinghy. At first, nothing happened even though my brother had the motor's throttle pegged full-open. After a few seconds, the sailboat started leaning a little more and started moving, then slid a little more, and suddenly it broke free of the stump and took off at full speed. Richard and I found ourselves riding in the dinghy, still tied to the top of the mast and being drug wildly backward through the wind and waves with water flooding in over its transom.

It was better than any amusement park ride I'd ever been on. Dad quickly swung the boat into the wind, halting the vessel and bringing our wild ride to, in my opinion a premature end. Once again, everything worked out except for Dad, who had to hear about it from my mother for a long time to come.

When my father eventually sold his sailboat, he asked my brother Richard if he would like to have the rubberized inflatable boat (RIB) that he used as a dinghy for the sailboat. Accepting it, Richard thought it would be fun to use exploring some of the rivers close to where we lived. Shortly after getting the RIB to Kentucky, he was ready to head out on his first river exploration. His son, Tripp, would man the RIB with him. Richard asked me to be part of the support crew.

Basically, I drove Richard, Tripp, the boat, and the trailer to the launch point in Rockport, Kentucky, and then I'd take the car and stay within a reasonable distance so that we could coordinate a take-out point.

While we were driving around and launching the RIB, no one noticed some ominous thunderclouds building on the horizon. Richard and Tripp had made it most of the way to Calhoun, Kentucky when the sky let loose. Water poured down in buckets, the sheets of rain so thick they could only see a foot or two in front of them.

As lightning flashed overhead and the wind howled, Richard headed in the direction of what he thought was the southern bank of the river. There he spotted a large tree to pull under for a little shelter. He and Tripp found a footpath on the bank, tied the RIB to the tree trunk, and headed up the footpath, looking for shelter. They came to a house with a bunch of people taking refuge on a screened-in porch. A man hollered to them to come on in and get out of the rain.

Richard discovered that the individuals on the porch were having a family reunion, and they invited him and Tripp to stay and have something to eat. My brother explained that they needed to get back to the boat and continue their trip as soon as the rain let up. The man told them they had gotten lucky and had just happened to find the last pullout on the river before the Calhoun Dam.

Sure enough, when they got back to the river, they saw that they had pulled the RIB out about fifty feet from the dam. It was a weir dam where the water ran over the top and then dropped about twenty feet straight down. If they had gone any further, they would have been swept over the dam and most likely drowned. Instead, they were invited to the family reunion of some nice people whom they had never met before and offered a meal! I give God credit for the save on this one. Once again, it strengthened my imperfect faith.

CHAPTER 11

Left in a Cave

I was fortunate to be raised by a father who loved sailing. When I was young, most of the vacations I went on were sailing trips with my Dad. When I was thirteen, we were in the Bahamas with some of his friends and one of my brothers. Wanting to find a certain cave on an island that he had read about, Dad asked me to go with him. We got in an inflatable dinghy and headed out. It was a bumpy ride. I was holding Dad's guidebook to the Bahamas, and it started to get wet as we bounced from wave to wave.

After about forty-five minutes of this, Dad finally found the cave. The water was plenty deep for us to float in, but the top of the cave entrance was only about two feet above the surface of the water. My father had to tilt the small outboard engine into the boat, and we were just barely able to squeeze into the cave.

Once inside, it was beautiful. The water was a shimmering turquoise blue. A hole opened in the roof of the cave about forty feet above us. It was approximately one foot in diameter, and the sun was shining through it like a spotlight. The entire interior of the cave was round and approximately sixty to seventy feet in diameter. The back of the cave had a small three-foot ledge, and everything was wet.

Handing me the guidebook and a slightly dry towel, Dad asked me to step on the ledge and dry the book while he went to find the sailboat and lead the rest of our group to the cave.

As I sat on the ledge, trying to dry the guidebook, I watched Dad squeeze under the roof to the mouth of the cave and disappear. Immediately I started thinking, what if Dad has a heart attack or something? No one knows where I am. That led to one fearful thought after another.

Then I noticed the water rising with the tide. The opening to the mouth of the cave grew smaller and smaller, and water started to wash onto the ledge. I panicked! The mouth of the cave was closing, and I didn't see any other way in or out. Certain that Dad would never find me, I started begging God for help. "Please don't let Dad have a heart attack! Please let him find the mouth of the cave and find me! Please stop the water rising!"

A few minutes later, I saw a snorkel pop up out of the water just inside the cave mouth. It was Mr. McCormick, a friend of my dad's. All my panic immediately went to thankfulness and then joy. I was saved!

Of course, I didn't realize it at the time; (which is why I panicked) that there was never anything to worry about. I spent all my time worrying myself sick instead of appreciating the beauty of the cave. God had known I was safe, and I had all this beauty I failed to notice because I had doubted Him. Of course, He was watching over me the whole time. He is always watching. There is no need to panic or waste precious time worrying. Once saved by Jesus Christ, you no longer need to worry about death. Just enjoy and live your life for God's glory.

CHAPTER 12

Frugal

On our way back from a sailing trip, we stopped at the West End in the Bahamas to have dinner and catch a flight. We planned to eat at the marina restaurant, which was notorious for having a large squadron of kamikaze mosquitos. Dad asked the restaurant manager if they still had the mosquito problem. The man assured him they didn't. He convinced Dad he was sincere by telling him our dinners would be on the house if we were bitten by one mosquito.

Dad then asked him if he could arrange to have a taxi pick us up and drive us to the airport in the morning. The manager explained that we wouldn't all fit in one regular taxi, he could get us two sedan taxis at $50 a piece, or we could get one van for $75. Dad asked him to have a van waiting for us no later than 8:30 am the next day. We ordered dinner and waited. By the time dinner arrived, we had each suffered at least 50 mosquito bites and used up an entire can of Off. After a few words between Dad and the manager, the meal was on the house.

The next morning, Kathy and I had our bags packed and on the dock, ready to go at 8:00 am on the dot. Plenty of time to grab a cup of coffee and catch the taxi. At 8:15 am, two sedan taxis pulled up. One of the drivers asked me if we were his fare to the airport. I told him we were waiting for a van. He looked at me puzzled, shrugged his shoulders, and got back in his cab.

Kathy told me to load our bags in the taxi so we could get to the airport so we didn't miss our flight. I told her I would check with dad to see if he was okay with us taking off.

Dad said, "No, we are going to wait for the van unless I just like burning $25."

I reported back to Kathy, who was not happy. It was a short ride to the airport, no more than twenty minutes, but our flight departed at 9:30 am, and she didn't think it was worth saving $25 to miss the flight.

Dad was having more words with the marina/restaurant manager and insisting that he get the van here and now.

The manager proceeded to make some calls and reported that the van was on the way.

I explained Kathy's logic to my dad and immediately received another lecture on the perils of wasteful spending. I clunked back over to Kathy. At his point, she was a nervous wreck. She begged me to put the luggage in the taxi. I told her I wasn't going to do it. I didn't want to be disrespectful to my dad, and we were going to wait for the van. After much begging, nervous sweating, and pacing back and forth on the dock, a van finally pulled up at about 9:10 am. If the driver hurried, we should just make it.

We took off down a pothole-filled road at about fifteen miles per hour. After a couple of blocks, the driver pulled up to a house, explaining that he had to pick up his wife to take her to work. After a couple of minutes inside the house, the driver came back out to the van tying a blue necktie on his white short-sleeve shirt. He was followed by his short and well-fed wife. At this point, it was about 9:20 am. Once again, we headed for the airport at a blistering fifteen miles per hour.

As we came up to the airport fence, I could see passengers walking up the portable stairs and loading up the small turbine airplane that we were about to miss. Dad and I ran into the airport. I got to the gate first and started begging the lady at the desk to hold the plane for us. She said she couldn't do it. I pointed out that the airplane door was still open; we were all here and ready to go, but she said she was sorry they had already shut the gate door, and there was nothing she could do. I begged and told her that dad and I were both million-mile gold and platinum cardholders with *American Airlines*, who travel extensively on AA for business; couldn't she do something? No matter what we said, she wouldn't budge.

Dad and I went to join the others, and I had to face Kathy. When we got outside, Dad noticed there was an airplane charter service next door. My dad had me check to see if we could secure a charter flight to Fort Lauderdale. I did it for the sum of $900. It was a decent twin-engine airplane; unfortunately, there were a few places where the floor in the plane had rusted through.

An unhappy Kathy could see the ocean beneath her feet while we flew to Fort Lauderdale. I did a lot of praying that morning. At this point, I was asking God to please get us to Fort Lauderdale alive.

We did arrive alive, and we saved $25 on our taxi fare, all while getting a free meal. And yes, I learned a lesson in frugality! Probably not the one Dad intended.

On the other hand, Kathy says the lesson I should have learned is that husbands should listen to their wives.

CHAPTER 13

Tempered Glass

When I was five years old, and my big brother was eight; we loved playing tag with dad. We would run after him laughing and giggling. He would race up and down the stairs, through the basement, and back up the stairs again. My older brother just about had him cornered when my dad jumped the railing and went flying down the stairs toward the front storm door.

When he hit the landing, he reached out for the door handle, expecting the door to open. His aim was off, so he missed the handle and went careening through the glass door, landing out on the front porch. I didn't at first realize what happened, then saw that a shard of glass had sliced through his calf.

My dad started yelling for my mother. She came running and immediately called for an ambulance and put a tourniquet on his thigh. Blood was everywhere, and he started turning pale. They took him away on a stretcher. My mother sat on the front porch with my brother and me, holding us tight and praying for God to take care of dad. The glass had cut a three-to-four-inch slice through his calf muscle, but fortunately missing all the tendons. The doctors sewed the calf up, and he was good to go in a few weeks.

As it happened, my dad was working for a window and door company and was on the technical committee of the aluminum window and door manufacturers' association. Also, serving on the safety sub-committee, he determined that what had happened to him wasn't going to happen to anyone else. Thus, he was instrumental in writing new national building codes and getting safety glass required on all doors and windows in unsafe locations.

God works in mysterious ways. I believe He made sure my father wasn't permanently maimed but scared enough to get the problem resolved. In this case, He used Dad to fix a big safety issue so that other fathers in the future wouldn't get hurt when playing with their kids. I'm sure thousands of people have been saved from serious injury, maiming, and even death as a result of taking our family's short-term misfortune and turning it into a long-term benefit for other families.

When your mother is praying for God to save your dad's life, you're not thinking, "I wonder if God will use this to fix a big problem for everyone." But keep your eyes open and watch Him work. It will amaze you.

CHAPTER 14

Work

If I'm honest about it, I was born with a tendency toward laziness. Fortunately, God had me born into a family in which my father wasn't going to accept such an attitude. I'd cringe to think how I would have ended up if my dad hadn't dedicated himself to making sure my brothers and I learned a work ethic.

I was eleven when my dad bought a farm with a valley and creek running through it. He loved racing hydroplane boats and said his intention was to build a lake where he could test boats of his own design. I'm convinced he really bought it to give me and my brothers projects to work on. When he ran out of things that we could do unsupervised, he had a large pile of rip rap stones delivered to the property and would have us place them by hand on the earthen dam.

When I asked him if we could use the tractor to move the stones, explaining it would make the work go much faster, he said, "John, I appreciate you using your brain and creatively thinking about more efficient ways to move the stone, but unfortunately you missed the point of the exercise. Now get back to work."

I now think the point was to work the lazy out of me (which it did). By the way, he was paying me .25 cents an hour. When I asked if I could go to work at the grocery as a bagger making $1.75 an hour in air conditioning with my friends, his simple answer was "no."

Dad bought the property in January. That month turned out to be a wet and frigid one. My first job was to hold a survey stick while Dad used the sextant. We were measuring the perimeter and elevation of what would be the lake shore. I would stand there holding the stick while he would shoot the reading. Every few minutes, I'd hear him shout for me to hold still so that he could get the reading. Of course, this was difficult for an eleven-year-old shivering in the cold drizzle.

My summer job was cutting down the trees in the valley with a chainsaw and attaching them with chains to the tractor so that my older brother could pull them out. Of course, being lazy, I told Dad that I didn't think it was fair my older brother got to drive the tractor all the time while I cut down the trees and hooked the logs.

"He's older, and he drives the tractor," my father would reply.

One day at the farm, I was cutting down trees and getting sloppy. The temperature was in the high nineties, and the humidity was worse. While sawing down one tree, it kicked up and hit the running chainsaw, and the chainsaw then hit my upper thigh. Now that woke me up. Freaked out, I could see where the running blade had cut right across the thigh of my blue jeans, leaving a gaping hole. But I didn't see any blood yet.

I kept looking and feeling my thigh through the hole. No blood? Somehow, I had managed to slice right through my jeans without leaving a scratch on me. Many times in my life, I've come close to serious injury, and I'm sure God has protected me.

I have friends and relatives who would read these stories and would say, "John, these things are just coincidences, serendipity, etc."

"You are welcome to look at it that way," I would reply, "but I choose to see time after time, I've been protected by God or given a path to take by Him for my benefit or others, and I know God is in it." I just have to continue working on my faith and being thankful even in times of despair, hoping He will let me see the good He plans to come from it so that I can experience the joy like my dad running through the glass door and then turning around and making everyone's home and office safer.

CHAPTER 15

Yankee Stadium

When Kathy and I lived in Connecticut, we took the children to see a ball game at Yankee Stadium. It was about a two-hour drive to New York City. We started back home around 10:00 pm. Unfortunately, I didn't know my way very well, and the navigation system in the car wasn't working properly. As a result, I blew past our exit for home. When I quickly started to pull over, Kathy began objecting vociferously. "What are you doing?"

"I'm going to back up and get on the ramp."

"NO, YOU ARE NOT!! You're going to kill us all!"

"No, I won't."

"I hope the police get you; you can't do this." she insisted.

"Calm down," I said, putting the car in reverse.

Immediately the blue light from a police motorcycle filled the car. I still have no idea where he came from.

"I told you so," Kathy announced. "I hope he puts you in jail!"

Six lanes of traffic zoomed by as the handsome black police officer with tall black motorcycle boots walked to our car. He indicated that I should roll down my window. As I did, Kathy started in a loud voice, telling him how she had told me not to do it and that she hoped he would arrest me or at least give me a ticket, etc. After requesting my driver's license, the Motorcycle officer then asked me what I was doing.

I explained the situation while my wife continued to request that he arrest and or at least ticket me. The officer then slowly handed me back my license while looking at Kathy and said, "Mr. Anderson, I think you have been punished enough this evening. Now if you wait here until I signal you, I'll stop the traffic so you can back up and get on the exit ramp."

When I glanced at Kathy's face, it was ashen white. The kids were sitting in the backseat, grinning ear to ear. The officer did exactly what he said he would, and we were on our way. To this day, I believe that officer was an angel sent by God. I still love NYC motorcycle police like brothers.

CHAPTER 16

Golf

One day Kathy came up with the idea that it would be fun if our family played golf together. I wasn't so sure. Still, while I wasn't a good golfer, I had been playing off and on for most of my adult life. My son, however, took one lesson and afterward announced that he didn't need anymore because he felt he now knew how to play. Kathy and my daughter, though, had never golfed before.

Deciding that the girls should compete against the guys, we put our stuff in the golf carts and headed to the first tee. My son and I teed off and managed to see that our balls were in play. After about ten tries, neither Kathy nor our daughter had managed to get off the tee box. They decided they would pick up their balls and place them somewhere "more convenient" in the fairway. Completely embarrassed, my son kept asking me to leave them behind. Though I was tempted, we soldiered on. Soon we saw the girls on the wrong fairway trying to hit their balls in the direction of some approaching golfers. At this point, I gave in to the temptation, and my son and I went and played another hole. After completing it, we decided to look for the girls and see how they were coming along.

Not far away, we saw them parked on a green and getting out to putt. I started driving toward them, yelling softly to get the cart off the green. Kathy sent our daughter to move the cart. She pulled it off the green and parked in front of the sand trap. When she got out of the cart, she didn't set the parking brake, and the vehicle started rolling backward, with both ladies screaming and running after it. After rolling a few yards, the cart jumped the curb and finally settled in the sand trap.

After my son and I retrieved the cart from the trap, I suggested we either quit now or maybe play the eighteenth hole since no other players were on it. At this point, I had been lecturing my wife and daughter about the rules and etiquette of golf, not driving on the greens or sand traps, hitting your ball the wrong way on fairways, etc. We were in the rough on the eighteenth fairway, and I was up. Kathy told me to be careful and not hit a fat oak tree between my ball and the eighteenth green.

Telling my wife not to worry about it, I explained that the tree was only about five percent of the airspace, and I would have a hard time hitting it even if I was trying to. "Fine," she replied.

Lining up the shot, I swung, hit the ball solidly, and it took off like a rifle shot directly for the tree. Hitting it square on, the ball ricocheted off, heading directly for me. I ducked for cover and fell to the ground, with the ball barely missing me.

Of course, this was hilarious to the girls, and they were laughing their heads off. Even my son found it pretty amusing. I felt betrayed.

At this point, no one had been hurt, and the golf course had not been significantly damaged, so I decided we should pick up our golf balls and head home. Once again, God had let me learn a valuable lesson about humility without allowing me to get physically hurt.

CHAPTER 17

Ducks

We moved to Coppell, Texas, for a new job right after our son, Preston, was born.

Just before we left, Kathy and I went to the fall festival at the school where she was a teacher. It was a Friday night. She was nine months pregnant. We had a nice time seeing all the parents and kids dressed up in costumes. Because Kathy was tired, we went home and straight to bed. At about 2:00 am, I could feel her shaking my arm, trying to wake me. Her water had broken. Our son was born the next evening. Monday, I flew to Texas to start my job.

That's right, we went to Kathy's last day at school on Friday, had our first baby on that Saturday, and I started a new job 750 miles away on Monday. I found a small rental house, and they joined me thirty days later. The house we eventually bought had a small park and pond about a block away. One day I took our three-year-old son, Preston, to the pond to go fishing.

It had a good population of ducks and geese on it. Unfortunately, they were not the least bit friendly. One time they even treed Kathy on top of a picnic table. I set Preston up sitting in his little red wagon with his fishing pole. The ducks were squawking up a storm. It sounded like, "Mack, Mack, Mack, Mack," and on and on. After a minute, my son looked at me and said, "Daddy?"

"What?" I answered,

He screwed up his little face. "Why are those ducks laughing at me?"

I tried hard not to burst out laughing myself, not wanting Preston to think that we were all laughing at him. Kids, in their innocence, are one of the greatest gifts God gives us. I now have grandchildren and just love seeing their smiles and the things they come up with.

There is nothing better than watching your children and grandchildren find their faith in God and his blessings.

CHAPTER 18

Angels

Our then two-and-a-half-year-old daughter, Raye, was asked to be in our church Christmas play. She was all excited about it until she found out she was going to be a sheep. Her best friend, Sarah, had been selected to be an angel. Raye had fallen in love with Sarah's costume with its gossamer wings and golden halo. No way did she want to be a fury sheep while Sarah was a beautiful angel.

In fairness, the sheep outfit was really cute, and Raye was adorable in it. It was time for the performance to start. Everyone thought she would be fine as a sheep. But she wasn't. She refused to walk into the sanctuary when it was her turn, thus blocking the door. Although her mother and Sunday school teacher kept trying to coax her in, she stubbornly refused to move. People in the pews started giggling and then laughing at the little sheep that wouldn't budge. Raye didn't care, they could laugh all they wanted.

Finally, Kathy asked me to go pick her up and set her on the stage so the play could go on. Raye is now the mother and angel to my two young grandsons, Jonah, two, and James, one.

CHAPTER 19

The Odd-shaped Dent

I moved our family to Connecticut for a new job I had just taken. We moved from Dallas, Texas, where it was often seventy degrees during January. I felt a little intimidated by the stories I had heard in which thirteen inch snowfalls were the norm. We had not been living in the state long when we experienced one.

A couple of days later, I was driving to work when I noticed that the stop sign on the corner not far from our house had been run over flat. Obviously, someone had lost control of their car, couldn't stop, and crashed into the sign. You could see where their tracks continued into the yard for a few feet. *That must have been scary,* I thought.

The next morning, I headed to work as usual. I opened the door from the mudroom into the garage, and as I stepped down, I noticed something odd on the front bumper of Kathy's van. It was a small U-shaped indentation, exactly the width and shape of the steel stop sign pole.

Walking back into the house, I said, "Kathy, have you seen this dent in the front bumper of the van?"

"What are you talking about?" she asked.

"I'm talking about the two-inch wide U-shaped dent in the front bumper that looks almost identical to the shape of the stop sign pole down the street that someone ran over."

Grinning ear to ear, Kathy put her hand over her mouth and burst out laughing.

The best medicine I've had while dealing with my disease is joyful outloud laughter shared with others. Even during the worst times, God is blessing us with gifts to be thankful for, like the laughter of a friend, a nice hot shower, or the warmth of the sun on your face. It can be difficult when we are feeling low, but we just need to see His gifts, be thankful, and experience the joy that comes with them.

CHAPTER 20

Rick

When I was in the fourth grade, I made friends with a boy called Rick. We were in the same classroom together, and he happened to live just down the street from our house. He would come over after school. My mother would give us a good snack, and we would go outside and play cowboys and Indians or Army with some of the other kids in the neighborhood. Rick and I both shared an interest in mechanical things and building stuff. We had the potential to become good pals.

Unfortunately, within a few days of becoming friends, Rick told me his family was moving. At the time, I didn't really understand the ramifications of this, but I soon learned it meant that he wasn't going to be available to play with me. His family left, and I moved on, not hearing from him again.

When I turned 57, I decided to buy an experimental airplane of tube and fabric construction. I had taken flying lessons when we lived in Connecticut and earned my private pilot's license. But I had never flown an airplane like the one I had purchased and had to have someone teach me how to fly it. I had built a grass runway in a field close to our house and found an instructor (Tommy) who would give me lessons.

Shortly the instructor told me he thought I was ready to fly solo, but he was going to be out of town for a few days. Then he explained that he knew a pilot who could get on the radio with me and talk me through it. "Great," I said.

Tommy phoned the pilot and gave him the location of my grass airstrip. Then Tommy called me and said the pilot would meet me at my field in thirty minutes. I headed to the field, getting a little nervous about flying solo for the first time without Tommy there and with a guy I had never met before talking me through it on the radio. A red experimental airplane soon showed up. His plane looked similar to mine, except mine was green. The guy did a few fancy flybys and came in for a landing.

In no time, he had taxied to the hangar where I was standing, stepped out of his airplane, and taken his helmet off. He looked at me a little funny, tilted his head to the side, and said, "John Anderson?"

I replied, "Yes,"

He said, "Remember me?"

"I'm not sure, but you look a little familiar."

"Rick, from fourth grade?"

"Oh. Yeah, hey, Rick, what are you doing here?"

"I'm the guy Tommy called to help you solo."

Turns out, Rick had moved a few times with his family and, after retiring from being a boilermaker, had built a house about a thirty-minute drive from where I had eventually constructed my home. And it was an eight-minute flight in my airplane. Rick and I instantly hit it off and picked up our friendship from fourth grade right where we had left off.

Most afternoons, I would make the eight-minute flight over to Rick's house, and we would sit around his hangar talking and working on projects together. It was a great blessing for me to have Rick back in my life, and we soon became best friends.

CHAPTER 21

Dining Table

My friend, Rick, has been there for me in many ways. To give you an idea of what kind of friend Rick is, I was in Florida receiving cancer treatments when he called and said he was coming down my way to go fishing. He wanted to know if he could stop by and say hi on his way back home.

"Absolutely, please do," I replied. We discussed a date and said goodbye. A few weeks later, he called to confirm the time he would be at the house. Kathy started putting together some cookies and sandwiches for lunch, and she invited her sister Annie to come over and meet Rick.

Then the two women started asking me if I thought he would have any room in his pickup to take back some stuff for us. "No, it wouldn't be right to impose on him," I protested. Rick showed up about 30 minutes later, pulling his fishing boat. Kathy and Annie came out and immediately inquired if he had any extra room and if he could take some stuff back to Kentucky for us.

"Sure, what is it?" he asked. They told him it was a large suitcase and an antique dining room table that Annie wanted to give to my daughter.

"No way, we aren't going to put that on Rick," I exclaimed. But he said it was fine, that he wanted to do it.

"What if it rains?" I questioned.

"It'll get wet," he said.

Annie didn't like that idea one bit.

But he said, "It isn't going to rain."

Checking her weather app, Annie decided it was a go. Rick put the suitcase in the crew cab of the truck, and then we spent the next hour driving to a storage facility and tying the table and a few dining room chairs into Rick's boat. Worried, I kept telling everyone, including Rick, that if it rained, it wasn't his fault. He still had a couple of stops to make to pick up strawberries and homemade peanut butter for his wife, so he got on his way.

Once he was on the road, he called his wife, Debbie, and told her what was up. "You know it's going to rain tonight?" she warned.

"When?"

"Looks like around 1:00 am."

Rick had planned on stopping halfway to get some rest, then finishing the rest of the way the next day. He immediately decided to drive straight through and try to beat the rain.

After about an hour, I called Rick to see how he was doing. Giving me an update on the rain; he said he planned to go straight through. I told him not to. "Don't worry about the table and chairs; I don't want you falling asleep at the wheel."

"I'll be fine," he insisted.

But as usual, I did worry and said a few prayers. Concerned, I also called him a few more times that evening to see how he was doing. The weather radar looked as if the rain was going to follow him all the way home. After an eleven-hour drive, he pulled his pickup and boat into his pole barn garage and unloaded the table and chairs. Fifteen minutes later, it started to pour. Again, I had spent a lot of energy and time worrying about nothing. I like to think the prayers helped.

My daughter now has a beautiful set of dining room chairs and table because of a good friend and anything God might have decided to do about the rain.

CHAPTER 22

The Missing Eyebrow

A few days after moving to Connecticut, I had a meeting scheduled in the morning with my boss, the owner of the company, and others. I have black eyebrows (reminiscent of Groucho Marx) that tend to get bushy if I don't use a trimmer on them. This particular morning, wanting to look my best, I grabbed the trimmer and didn't notice the trim guard had fallen off. I proceeded to shave my right eyebrow completely off. Because it didn't get any sun, the skin under the eyebrow was untanned white.

When I looked in the mirror, I felt sick to my stomach! What was I going to do? I called for Kathy, and she came running. "Look at what I've done!" I exclaimed.

Her eyes went wide with dismay. Then she started to giggle, then laugh, and finally fell on the bed, holding her stomach and crying with laughter. After all, I did look pretty ridiculous, with one black eyebrow and one white. I was worried sick about the impression I would make at my new job, figuring that if I told them what I'd done, they would fire me on the spot for being too stupid to handle the responsibilities they had given me.

After a few minutes of me worrying and Kathy laughing, she said, "Come in the bathroom and let me put some makeup on it." She did, but I still looked like a guy who had shaved off one of his black eyebrows and whose wife's attempt at covering it with makeup had not worked out so well. It was horrible. For a moment, I thought I was just going to have to call in sick for a few weeks until it grew back. But, no, I couldn't do that with a new job!

Then Kathy said, "I know. We'll put a band-aid on it."

"What? How will I explain that?"

"Just tell them you had something removed. You don't have to tell them it was your eyebrow."

Unable to think of a better idea, we put on a skin-colored band-aid, and I headed out to work, worrying all the way and feeling physically sick. I was also praying that God could find some way to help me. Praying is my go-to habit during times of stress. Finally, I pulled into the office parking lot. My skin was clammy with a bead of sweat on my brow; I was on the verge of dry heaves, certain my family's future was at stake.

Opening the office door, I said "Hi" to the receptionist. She tilted her head slightly, hesitated a fraction of a second, and said with a nice smile, "Good morning." My meetings went well, and nobody said a thing about the band-aid. I figured they were either used to people shaving their eyebrows off or were too polite to mention the band-aid.

At the end of that day, I met with my boss. After a few minutes, he said, "What happened to your eye?"

"Oh, I had something removed."

"Oh," he replied. And that was that.

Once again, I had wasted a bunch of time and energy, completely stressed out for no reason. See a pattern?

CHAPTER 23

Smoke

One day Kathy called me at work to tell me she thought the van had caught on fire and now wouldn't run. She said white smoke was billowing out of the exhaust pipe. It turned out a gasket had failed, and anti-freeze was pouring into the engine. The smoke had become so thick in the garage that she couldn't see.

It was winter in Connecticut, and Kathy had loaded the kids into the van to drive them two houses down the street where the school bus would pick them up. When she started the van, white smoke filled the garage. Now, as I later explained to Kathy, at this point, most reasonable people would turn the van off and then walk the kids the short distance to the bus stop. But not Kathy. Pushing the garage door opener, she backed out of the garage and then proceeded to the bus stop with plume white smoke trailing her. It looked like some sort of mosquito-fogging truck. Our five-year-old daughter, too embarrassed to be seen by her friends, crawled under the seat.

Shortly the engine seized and I got a phone call from Kathy. I contacted the Ford dealer in town. They picked up the van, gave us a loaner, and returned the vehicle a couple of weeks later with a brand-new engine and no bill. (I've been a fan of Ford ever since then). Eventually, I told Kathy, "If the van starts smoking again, please shut it off and call me before doing anything else." She promised she would.

I believe God was watching out for them that day.

CHAPTER 24

What Was That?

I was in our kitchen in Connecticut with the kids when we heard a crash out in the garage. All three of us ran to the door to see what had happened. Kathy had backed the van into the closed garage door. She explained that she had pushed the wrong garage opener button. After she heard my garage door open, she put the van in reverse and rammed it into her door.

The kids were laughing away while I gave her grief for not being more cautious. "Can't you check your rear-view mirror before backing up?"

Now the garage door wouldn't open. I had to disengage the mechanism and was just able to lift the door up manually so that she could get out. That night I came home, hit my garage door opener, and saw Kathy's van parked in my space. I got out of the car, went through the process of manually opening her door, and parked my car in her space.

The next morning after breakfast, giving Kathy a kiss and telling the kids to have a good day at school, I went out in the garage, got in my car, hit the garage door opener, and heard my door going up. Forgetting that I had parked in Kathy's space the night before, I then proceeded to back into the garage door, finishing the job of destroying it that Kathy had started. Of course, she and the kids came running to the garage to see what had happened. The kids thought it was hilarious, at least ten times funnier than when mom had done it. They were laughing themselves into tears as Kathy proceeded to ask me why I wasn't more cautious. "Don't you check your rear-view mirror before backing up?"

Epilogue

We have been fighting this brain cancer for sixteen months now. The average lifespan for someone diagnosed with this tumor is eight months post diagnosis. My doctor took me off chemotherapy because I had difficult side effects. I'm still participating in the clinical trial getting either a placebo vaccine or the real thing every five weeks. We have had five MRIs to see if any new tumors have started. So far, Dr. Tran says my MRI scans are "fantastic." What's next? We keep an eye on it.

I try not to worry, knowing God is present with me regardless of what happens. He, in His glory, will make some good come from it, and I try to make the most of every minute of the life He has left for me. Hopefully, it will include a lot of teasing, laughter, and fun, like when my friends Mike and Howdy called for an update. Mike said, "John, what did they find on the scans?"

I replied, "Nothing."

"I knew it," he said. "They could have saved a lot of time and money if they had just asked me. I could have told them any brain scan of yours would obviously show nothing." I cracked up until I had tears in my eyes.

God has been present in my life from the beginning. Fortunately, I started to recognize His presence when I was ten-years-old. During this challenge, my family and I have continued to see Him work in our lives. I know He is keeping an eye on me and supporting me when I need Him most. He will do the same for you. Just keep your eyes open, and when you see Him working in your life, take a minute to thank Him and appreciate the blessings that come from a grateful heart.

I hope from reading these stories; you will see how each story could have been a disaster or a blessing, for example, "I have terminal cancer," or "God has blessed me and helped me write a book." God gave us the miracle of life and the free will to see His miracle how we choose. He also gave us the best gift of all, His Son, who suffered, died, and was resurrected, so that we can be worthy of a relationship through eternity with Him without the burden of our sin. All He asks is that we accept Jesus Christ/His Son as our Savior and repent of our sins. Ask yourself, "Did I just get hit by another catastrophe, or do I need to be patient, open my eyes, and see how God just blessed me?" You will suffer, though nothing like how Jesus suffered for you. Remember, with Jesus Christ as your Savior, the end of the story is always good!

Author Bio

John Anderson was raised in Kentucky and enjoys football and basketball. He has earned his private pilot's license and has flown everything from a kite to experimental aircraft. He also has multiple certifications in scuba diving. He is an avid cyclist and enjoys long walks with his wife and friends. He loves sailing and being on blue water close to white sand beaches.

9 781958 000427